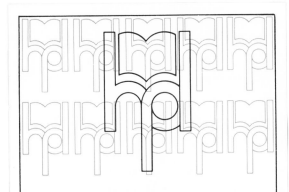

When it is Night, When it is Day

Jenny Tyers

Houghton Mifflin Company

Boston New York

1996

jPic
Tye

First American edition 1996 published by Houghton Mifflin Company
First published in Australia by Penguin Books Australia Ltd.

For information about this and other Houghton Mifflin trade and reference
books and multimedia products, visit The Bookstore at Houghton Mifflin on
the World Wide Web at (http://www.hmco.com/trade/).

Manufactured in Australia
The text of this book is set in 24–point Bodoni.
The illustrations are etchings reproduced in full color.

10 9 8 7 6 5 4 3 2 1

Library of Congress Cataloging-in-Publication Data
Tyers, Jenny.
When it is night, when it is day / by Jenny Tyers.– 1st American ed.
p.   cm.
Summary: The sounds and activities of nocturnal animals are contrasted
with those of animals that are awake during the day.
ISBN 0-395-71546-6
[1. Night—Fiction. 2. Day—Fiction. 3. Animals—Fiction.] 1. Title
PZ7.T936Wh 1996 [E]—dc20 94–19925 CIP AC

To R. B. and Snowy
— J. T.

When it is NIGHT

When it is night,

the llama shuts its eyes.

The wolf howls.

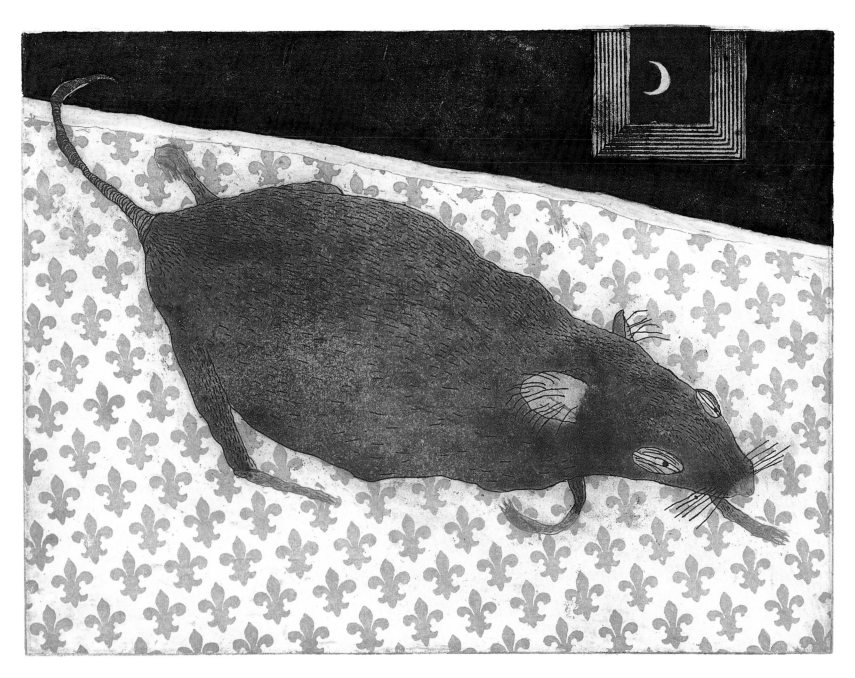

The mouse skitters.

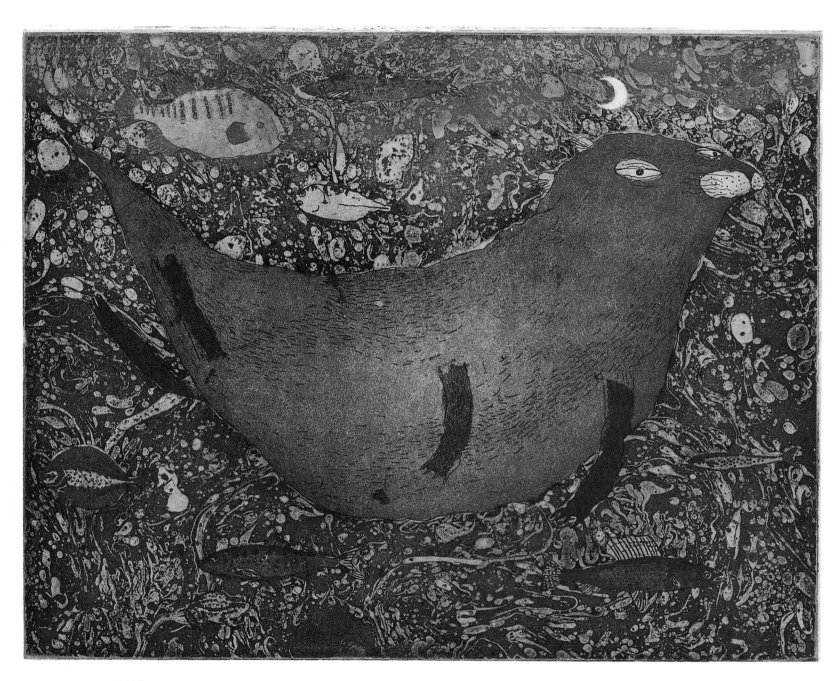

The otter swims.

The armadillo digs.

The cat prowls.

The frog croaks.

The owl hoots.

The bat swoops.

The rooster crows.

The llama opens its eyes.

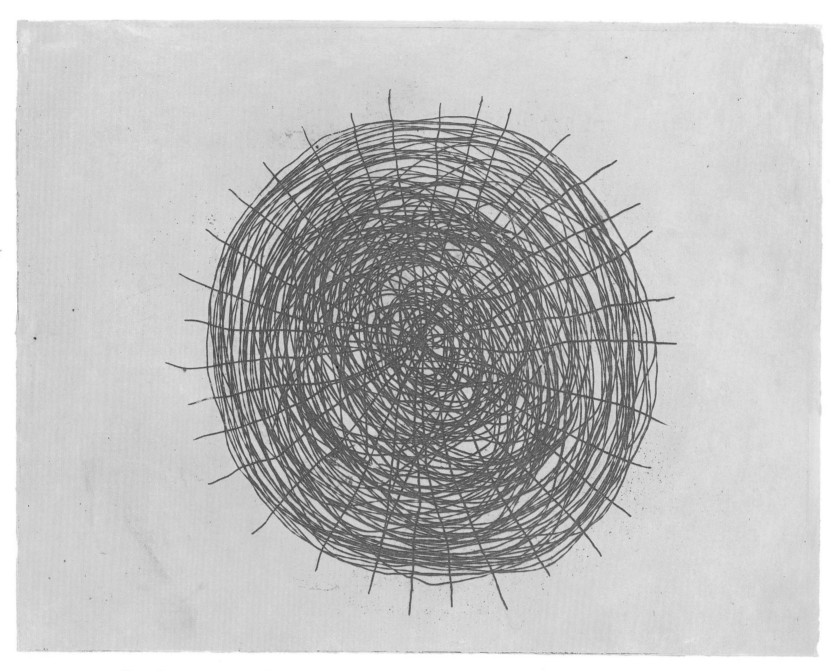

It is morning.

When it is DAY

When it is day,

the hedgehog shuts its eyes.

The cow chews.

The monkey swings.

The fox runs.

The rhinoceros munches.

The squirrel collects.

The wart hog snuffles.

The bear fishes.

The antelope leaps.

The hare comes out to eat.

The hedgehog opens its eyes.

It is night.